RUNNING
OUT OF TIME

by ELIZABETH LEVY

Illustrated by W. T. Mars

ALFRED A. KNOPF : NEW YORK

Other Knopf Capers books

Man from the Sky by Avi
Rosie's Double Dare by Robie H. Harris
The Case of the Weird Street Firebug by Carol Russell Law
The Mystery on Bleeker Street by William H. Hooks
The Robot and Rebecca by Jane Yolen

This is a Borzoi Book
Published by Alfred A. Knopf, Inc.

10 9 8 7 6 5 4 3 2

Library of Congress Cataloging in Publication Data

Levy, Elizabeth. Running out of time
   (Capers)
Summary: While running in the fog early one morning,
three friends suddenly find themselves in the Roman Empire
of 73 B.C. where they become catalysts in a slave revolt led
by the gladiator Spartacus. 1. Spartacus, d. 71 B.C.—
Juvenile Fiction. [1. Spartacus, d. 71 B.C.—Fiction.
2. Slavery in Rome—Fiction. 3. Gladiators—Fiction.
4. Space and time—Fiction. 5. Rome—History—
Servile War, 73–71 B.C.—Fiction] I. Title.
PZ7.L5827Es [Fic] 79–28064
ISBN 0–394–84422–X pbk.
ISBN 0–394–94422–4 lib. bdg.

To George with love

Contents

RUNNING OUT OF TIME

1

The Fog

NINA TIPTOED past her parents' room. The house was dark—too dark. It was just before dawn, but even so there should have been more light. Fred, Nina's English sheep dog, kept snapping playfully at her loose shoelaces.

"Hush!" warned Nina. She hoped her parents wouldn't wake up. She pulled the laces tight and headed for the front door. Fred followed her silently.

Outside, the driveway and the road looked spooky in an early morning ground fog. "It'll burn off," Nina said to herself hopefully as she ran down the road.

Last year, when she was ten, Nina had been the youngest girl in the state to complete a marathon, running 26.2 miles in a little under four hours. This year she wanted to better her time, and she was training hard. Francie and Bill, two of Nina's best friends, had decided to train for the marathon, too.

Bill was waiting outside, doing some last-minute stretches on his lawn.

"Hi," he said, looking around anxiously. "The fog's strange, isn't it?"

"It keeps the air cool," said Nina, matter-of-factly. "That's what I like."

Bill and Nina began running side by side. "How far are we going to run today?" Bill asked. Nina was in charge of their training schedule.

"I think we'll do an eight-mile run," she said, looking down at her wrist watch, which could tell time to the 100th of a second.

"I don't think Francie is going to like that," said Bill.

"If she wants to run the marathon in October, she's got to pick up her mileage," said Nina.

"What won't Francie like?" said a voice through the fog. Fred began to bark. Then Francie suddenly appeared. Her curly hair bounced around her face.

"You scared me," Bill said.

"I was hiding in the fog," said Francie. "I could hear you talking all the way down the road, but you couldn't see me. Isn't this fog neat? It almost makes running fun."

"I don't like it," Bill replied. "I think it's very weird."

"Who knows what evil lurks . . . in the fog. . . ." boomed Francie in a low voice.

Nina laughed. "Just be grateful that it's not hot," she said. Nina picked up the pace. Francie and Bill kept up with her, but it wasn't easy. They ran for about a mile without talking. Fred ran ahead.

"The fog isn't burning off," Bill observed. "If anything, it's getting thicker."

"I tell you," said Nina, "this weather is

great for running. Don't you feel terrific?"

"To tell the truth," Francie admitted, "I'm still tired from yesterday's run."

Nina gave her a concerned look. "If you're really tired, you shouldn't overdo it. Nobody's making you train."

"I know," said Francie, "but since I've started running, I can eat all the pizza I want, and I am actually losing weight. I'm hooked on running."

"You're just hooked on pizza," said Bill.

"I'd rather run than give up pizza," said Francie. "That's how much I love pizza."

Bill shrugged his shoulders impatiently.

Francie was surprised. Usually, Bill was very good-natured, very calm. "Hey, Bill," she asked, "why are you in such a bad mood?"

"I guess it's the fog," he said. "I've never seen fog like this. It gives me the creeps.

Besides, I still haven't thought up a history project." Bill was a grade-A student and also a grade-A worrier. History was his best subject, but that didn't stop him from worrying about it.

"I'm doing a project on the first marathon runner in ancient Greece," said Nina. "He ran all the way from Sparta to Athens, twenty-six miles, and then he died."

"Yeah," said Francie. "It can be a short paper."

"What's your project—'Great Pizzas in History'?" asked Nina.

"That's not a bad idea," said Francie. "I'd love the research. I could eat a slice from every country."

"Pizza was invented in the United States," said Bill, "in nineteen forty-seven."

Francie playfully stuck out her tongue at Bill. "You would know something like that," she said, beginning to breathe hard. They were running up a long hill. Because Nina was the best runner, she began to pull ahead. Fred bounded up the hill as if it were nothing. Francie wished she had four legs. She and Bill ran side by side. Within seconds Nina was lost in the fog, but they could still hear her footsteps.

"This fog just keeps getting worse and worse," said Bill gloomily. Francie no longer felt like making jokes. She was panting hard. She was afraid that if she didn't keep up, she would be all alone in the fog.

"Nina," she shouted, "don't get too far ahead. We can't see you."

In the distance, Francie and Bill heard Fred bark nervously. Francie looked around. The fog was so thick she could barely see Bill, and he was only a few feet away from her.

"It's eerie. . . . I don't like this fog any more," said Francie anxiously. She peered into the heavy mushroom-soup fog all around them and shivered. She was scared but she didn't know why.

2

Back in Time

NINA FELT the change first. Suddenly the road beneath her feet switched from black asphalt to hard rounded stones. The feeling under her feet was so strange that she stopped short. There were no stone roads around Denver where they lived, and she was sure she had not made a wrong turn. The fog seemed to be getting even thicker.

"Francie! Bill!" shouted Nina. No one answered. Nina whirled around as she felt something furry brush against her leg. It was only Fred. She patted his side in relief. Nina was hardly ever frightened, but she was now. Finally, she heard two voices yelling, "Nina! Nina!"

"I'm here!" she shouted back. Francie and Bill appeared as dim figures in the fog.

"What happened to the road?" asked Francie.

"We must have made a wrong turn in the fog," Bill said.

"We did not," insisted Nina. The fog had started to lift, and it was becoming warmer. Bill, Nina, and Francie stared in shock as the landscape came into view. In place of the Aspen trees that lined the roads in Colorado, there were rows and rows of olive trees. And the road was paved with stones tightly fitted together. It was a beautifully made road, wide and built higher than the surrounding land. Nina, Bill, and Francie were speechless. They could not believe their eyes.

Nina glanced down at her arm. "My watch!" she cried. "It's gone!"

"Look at our clothes!" shrieked Francie.

Instead of their regular running shorts and tops, all three were dressed in short tunics

made from the same rough, grayish-white
cloth.

"Help!" screamed Francie, turning in
circles. "Help!"

"Shut up!" Nina snapped. "We've got to
figure out what's going on. Yelling won't do
any good."

"How do you know?" demanded Francie.
"Maybe yelling will do a lot of good."

"Stop arguing," Bill said. He looked down

12

at himself. "You don't have it so bad. Look at me. I'm in a dress!"

"It's more like a mini-skirt," said Francie.

"It's like we're all having the same dream," Nina mused.

"Or nightmare," said Francie, sitting down on a large stone by the side of the road. The stone was about two feet high and had a flat top.

"Quick! Get off that stone," said Bill.

"I wish you two would stop ordering me around," Francie grumbled. "I'm not moving. This is all too weird for me."

"There's something written on that stone," said Bill. "If you get off, we can look at it."

Francie jumped up, and the three of them looked carefully at the stone. Written on its side, in large square-cut letters, were the following words:

VIA APIA
CAPUA·IX
ROMA·CLV.
POMPEII XX

"It's a milestone!" exclaimed Bill.

"Terrific," said Francie. "I'm glad to know this crazy event is a milestone in our lives." Francie shook her head. She turned to Bill. "Will you stop talking like you're giving a speech!"

"I mean this is a real Roman milestone," said Bill. "The Romans were the greatest road-builders of all time. We're on the Appian Way!"

Francie and Nina stared at him as if he had gone out of his mind. Bill was too excited to notice.

"Luckily I can read Roman numerals," he said.

"Lucky," muttered Francie. Bill got down on his hands and knees to look closely at the milestone.

"We're a hundred and fifty-five miles from Rome and only twenty miles from Pompeii," he said.

"Great," said Francie. "I always wanted to run to Pompeii. I hear they have terrific pizza."

14

"We're only nine miles from Capua, wherever that is."

"How did we get to Rome?" demanded Nina. "This is insane. What's happening? Where's my watch? Why are we dressed like this?"

"How are we going to get back?" shouted Francie.

"I don't think we're in Italy," said Bill. "Italy doesn't exist yet. Look at that milestone. It's brand new. Look at the clothes we're wearing. Everything about us from the twentieth century is gone."

"I've heard of runner's high," joked Francie, "but this is ridiculous."

"Are you saying that fog carried us back in time?" Nina asked.

"I'm as confused as you are," said Bill. "I just know that is a *real* Roman milestone, and this is a Roman road."

"What's that?" asked Francie on guard, whirling around.

Fred barked. They could hear the sound of many footsteps. Soon they saw a group of men and boys, dressed in the same short tunics, running toward them. Nina thought they looked like the top runners back in the United States—thin but healthy. Then she saw that many of their bodies were criss-crossed with deep scars.

A man on a beautiful white horse rode beside them, sometimes forcing them to run faster. He snapped a huge whip at anyone who slowed down.

Suddenly he stopped right in front of Nina, Francie, and Bill.

"Why are you standing there?" he asked.

"What?" stammered Francie, looking at the whip in horror. Before she had been scared because things were so odd. Now she was terrified. She looked at Nina and Bill. Bill was shaking. Nina stood perfectly still, almost like a statue. Francie couldn't tell whether Nina was scared or not.

"Get moving," demanded the man on the horse. "I didn't give you permission to rest."

"You don't understand," said Nina, moving closer to the man to explain. "We . . ."

She never got to finish her sentence.

"I'm not interested in excuses," said the man. Then he snapped his whip over their heads. Without even thinking, Francie and Bill ducked. But that just made Nina very angry. "Stop trying to scare us with that horrible whip," she said.

"He's not just trying," whispered Francie. "I think he's succeeding."

"How dare you speak back to me?" said the man.

"We're sorry, sir," stammered Bill. "We're new here."

"Let's just do what he says. We can find out what's going on later," whispered Francie.

The man on the horse climbed down and walked toward them menacingly. "I'll teach you three young gladiators to respect me."

"Stop threatening us!" shouted Nina.

"Nina," whispered Bill urgently, "I don't think this is a good place to pick an argument."

"He's a bully," Nina protested.

"Yeah," said Francie, "a bully with a whip. That's the worst kind."

"Until we figure out what's going on, I think we should go along with him," whispered Bill.

"He doesn't seem like the type who'd listen to reason," said Francie.

The man snapped his whip close to Nina's feet. Nina jumped. Fred whimpered.

"Well!" demanded the man. "Are you going to move?"

Nina gave him a nasty look. But she decided she'd better jog down the road behind the gladiators. Francie and Bill followed her. Fred ran by their side. The man with the whip smiled and mounted his horse.

3

Don't Act Frightened

THE GROUP of gladiators seemed to slow their pace to let Nina, Francie, and Bill catch up with them.

"You were very brave to talk back to Marcus," whispered a young boy about their age.

"Is that his name?" asked Nina. "He's a brute."

"Where are you from?" asked the boy. "I don't remember you at the barracks. You must have just arrived."

"Uhh . . . it's hard to explain where we're from," said Nina, looking around at Francie and Bill for help. Francie shook her head as

if to say, Don't ask me how to explain this nightmare.

"I'm Britanicus," said the boy. "I was wondering if you were from Britain, too. We have dogs like yours tending our sheep at home."

Nina smiled. "Good old Fred. He's an English sheepdog all right. But we're not from England."

"Fred?" said Britanicus. "What a strange name for a dog. What is your name?"

"Nina. And these are my friends Francie and Bill."

Both Francie and Bill managed weak smiles.

"More strange names," said the boy. "But we gladiators come from all over the world. The Romans pick us from the best and strongest of their slaves." He sounded very proud.

"We are *not* slaves," insisted Nina.

"Shhh," whispered Bill, worried that

Nina would get them in trouble again.

Britanicus smiled. "You certainly tried to act free when you spoke back to Marcus."

Bill decided to interrupt before Nina became indignant again. "How far will they make us run?" he asked, grateful that they were in good shape.

"Nine miles. Our barracks are in Capua," said Britanicus.

Nina glanced back at Francie anxiously. Nine miles was farther than either Francie or Bill should be running at this stage of their training.

Nina slowed her pace to run beside her friend. "Are you all right?" she whispered.

"I'm okay," said Francie grimly. "I just hate running with a whip over my head. I'm scared."

"Me too," admitted Nina. She turned to Bill. "How about you? Are you okay?"

"I think so," he said. "Just our luck. We travel back in time and we come back as slaves."

"Are gladiators slaves?" asked Francie,

22

glancing at the scars on Britanicus's body. "I thought gladiators were warriors."

"No. They were slaves who were forced to fight each other, sometimes to the death," said Bill. "The Romans liked to watch them the way we watch football players."

Francie shuddered. "That's disgusting."

Britanicus fell into step with them again. "You've got to be careful about talking so loud," he warned. "Marcus doesn't like that."

Just then, a small man with deep-set eyes and black hair ran alongside them. At first glance he looked tough and cruel. Then he smiled at Nina, Francie, and Bill, and his face changed completely.

"These three children are very brave," he said to Britanicus. "I liked the way they stood up to Marcus. They put the rest of us to shame." Then he dashed on ahead.

"Who's that?" whispered Francie.

"Spartacus," said Britanicus. "He's the best gladiator in our school." Britanicus seemed to be in awe of the small man.

They ran in silence for a while. Francie felt like crying. What in the world could have happened to them in that fog? They had lost all ties with the twentieth century. They could speak and understand Latin. But they could still remember everything about the twentieth century. Francie wondered whether they would ever see home again. If this was a nightmare, Francie wanted to wake up.

Lost in her thoughts, Francie stumbled and fell. She scraped her hands on the stone road. Looking down at the small bloody scratches on her palms, she suddenly knew for certain that this was *not* a dream. She wiped her hands on her tunic and started to cry.

Nina and Bill ran to her side.

"Get up," whispered Nina.

"I want to go home," Francie sobbed quietly.

"You have to get up," urged Nina.

Marcus halted his horse in front of them and got down. He cracked his whip in the air.

"Here comes the whip-snapper," said Bill. "Francie, get up!"

"I can't. I'm too tired," she moaned. "I don't think I can run any longer."

"*I'll* help you get up," said Marcus, raising his whip in the air. But before he could strike Francie, someone grabbed his arm. It was Spartacus.

"Spartacus, how dare you?" growled Marcus.

"This boy is new," said Spartacus. "He's running as hard as he can. Do you want to waste your master's money by spoiling a young gladiator? Someday this boy might win your master a lot of money."

"*Boy?*" whispered Francie in horror. "He thinks we're boys. What's going to happen when they find out Nina and I are girls?"

"Shhh," whispered Bill. "That's the least of our problems now."

Spartacus held out his hand to help Francie. Marcus watched angrily. "This is the second time this group of young gladiators has stopped without my permission," he said.

"I fell," said Francie. "I didn't stop on purpose."

Spartacus moved in front of Francie as if to protect her.

"I myself will help train these children," said Spartacus. "You won't have to worry about them."

Marcus lowered his whip. "See that we don't have to stop for them again," he commanded. He whirled his horse around and rode to the front of the column.

Spartacus smiled at Francie, Nina, and Bill. "Run beside me, boys," he said. "And don't act frightened."

"Easier said than done," Francie mumbled.

"As for me, I'm scared stiff," agreed Bill. Even Nina nodded.

⎍⎍⎍⎍⎍⎍⎍⎍⎍⎍⎍⎍⎍⎍⎍⎍⎍⎍⎍⎍⎍⎍⎍⎍⎍

4

Slaves in the City

THE SUN felt hot, much hotter than the Denver sun. Nina could feel the sweat pouring off her back. She was thirsty, but Marcus forced them to keep running. Suddenly the road turned slightly, and in the distance Nina could see a huge wall.

"That must be Capua," said Bill.

Nina nodded. "I hope we get to stop and have a drink soon," she said, her mouth dry.

As they got closer to the town, they passed more and more merchants and farmers who barely gave the gladiators a second look. Once in a while a wealthy young woman would go by, carried in a chair by six slaves. The women looked at the gladiators admiringly. One young woman even threw flowers in their direction.

A flower landed in Nina's hair, and the young woman, only a few years older than Nina, smiled happily and waved.

"You have a wealthy admirer," said Britanicus, laughing. "Maybe she'll cheer you in the arena."

Nina brushed the flower from her hair angrily. "I'm not going to fight to amuse some spoiled brat who makes other people carry her around." Nina almost spat out the words.

Britanicus looked puzzled. "But that is the custom," he said.

"Is that wall the city of Capua?" asked Bill, hoping to change the subject.

"Of course," said Britanicus. "Haven't you seen it before?"

Bill didn't know what to answer. Luckily, Francie picked up the ball. "Why is it so big?" she asked.

"You only see half the wall," said Britanicus. "It goes down thirty feet below the ground. That way, enemies attacking the city can't tunnel underneath and into it."

"And no slave can escape out of it," added Spartacus bitterly. He had come up to run beside them. "I know there is something strange about you three," he whispered. "Be careful. We will find a time to talk later," he added with a smile. Francie felt slightly reassured.

Marcus allowed the gladiators to slow to a

walk as they approached the gates. The heavy wooden doors of the gates were covered with bronze and swung open for them.

As they walked through the gates, Nina, Francie, and Bill stared in wonder. Each block was lined with stores, restaurants, and houses. Much to Nina, Francie, and Bill's surprise, there were apartment houses, some nearly five stories high.

"Look at the fountain!" yelled Nina,

dashing over to a beautifully carved stone fountain. She put her whole face in the fountain, gladly lapping up the cool water.

Marcus allowed all the gladiators to drink. Every block had its own public fountain, where people too poor to have running water in their homes could get fresh water.

They walked along the sidewalks of Capua. Many of the townspeople waved at them as if they were famous.

Francie waved back. "I guess being a gladiator is a great thing," she giggled.

Bill shook his head. "Just remember that we're slaves," he warned.

A group of young men passed by, shouting, "Spartacus! Spartacus!" Spartacus stared straight ahead, paying no attention to their shouts.

"They will shout just as loudly for the gladiator who kills me," he said bitterly. Now there was no trace of a smile of his face.

In the shadow of a huge oval amphitheater Marcus called the gladiators to a halt. "That is where we fight," whispered Britanicus.

"Our barracks are right next to the amphitheater." He pointed to a group of low wooden buildings, all facing a large courtyard.

"What happens now?" whispered Nina.

"We eat breakfast," Britanicus said. "Stick with me. I'll show you what to do."

Nina reached out for Francie's hand, and Francie took Bill's. They didn't want to get separated. All the gladiators headed straight for low benches alongside the cookhouse.

"I wonder what we're going to get to eat?" asked Francie. "I hope it's not too yuccky. I wish you hadn't told me pizza wasn't invented yet."

"I bet it'll be either bread or some kind of cereal," said Bill. "I remember reading that the Romans had huge supplies of grain that they took from all the countries they conquered."

A woman silently placed a bowl of porridge in front of each of them. Nina, Francie, and Bill looked into their bowls curiously.

"It looks like hot cereal," said Nina.

"I hate hot cereal," said Bill. "I never eat it at home."

Nina put a little bit on her spoon. What if it were poison? What if their bodies couldn't take the change. The spoon hovered in the air.

"Oh, for goodness' sake," said Francie. "I'm hungry." And she swallowed a large spoonful. "It's delicious!" she cried. "It's got honey and raisins in it."

Nina and Bill dug into their porridge happily. Francie ate all of hers, but she was still hungry. She looked around, afraid to ask for more, but then a tall slave with jet black hair and piercing eyes to match came quickly to her side. She ladled more porridge into Francie's bowl. The woman seemed very stern. But then her eyes met Francie's, and she smiled. Her smile lit up her whole face, and her manner reminded Francie of Spartacus.

"Eat as much as you like, child," whispered the woman. She poured more porridge into Nina's and Bill's bowls as well.

"I am Cipriana, Spartacus's wife," she whispered. "He told me that you children somehow got lost and were caught by Marcus. Don't be afraid. We will see that you are safe."

"Please, ma'm," said Nina timidly. "Could I have some food for my dog. Poor Fred. He hasn't had anything to eat all day."

Fred wagged his tail weakly at the sound of his name. He was lying down underneath the table.

Cipriana put down a bowl of porridge for Fred and patted him on the head. "I'll see if we have any meat scraps in the kitchen. He seems like a nice dog, and I know how much

it means to have a pet from home with you." Then she moved on to serve more porridge to the other gladiators.

"I wonder what she would think if she knew just how lost we were," Francie whispered to Bill.

"I just wish I knew how we're going to get back," said Bill with a sigh.

"This has to be a dream, doesn't it?" whispered Nina.

"I don't know what it is," said Francie, "but I know it's not a dream. When I fell, I really hurt myself. If it was a dream, I'd be awake and back in Denver by now."

"I think it had to be something in the fog," said Nina. "When we run, our bodies change and we use oxygen better. Something in that fog must have mixed with our blood to send us back in time. Einstein had a theory that time would stand still if you could go as fast as the speed of light. Some people have said that if you could go faster than the speed of light, you could go back in time."

"Come on, Nina, you're fast, but you're not that fast," said Bill.

"Who cares about the speed of light," said Francie. "I just want to get back home."

Bill looked at her, close to despair. "I haven't the foggiest idea how to get back home," he whispered.

"We just have to find that fog again," said Nina. "Then we'll get back to Denver."

"We don't know that for sure," said Bill sadly. "We could be stuck here forever."

5

Spartacus Learns the Truth

AFTER BREAKFAST, guards herded the gladiators into the open courtyard to begin their daily practice. Nina, Francie, and Bill stood in a corner, hoping that no one would notice them.

"What are we supposed to do now?" Nina whispered to Britanicus. All around them, men moved quickly, picking up swords and shields.

Spartacus came over. He was carrying a small round shield and a sharp curved dagger shaped like a wild boar's tusk.

He poked the dagger at Francie playfully. She jumped and screamed. Everyone stopped to look around. The guards began to suspect something.

"It's nothing. It's nothing," Spartacus told the guards. "I was just going to give these young gladiators the first lesson using the Thracian sword."

The guards grunted and went back to watching the other gladiators. "I'm sorry I scared you," whispered Spartacus. "You acted as if you had never seen a Thracian dagger before."

"I haven't," exclaimed Francie, bursting into tears. The strain of the morning had finally gotten to her.

"It's just made of wood," said Spartacus, holding out the dagger so that Francie could look at it more closely. "They only allow us to use real swords when we go into the arena."

"You're going to find this hard to believe," said Francie, trying to sniff back her tears, "but back in Denver my mom doesn't let me play with daggers."

"Denver?" said Spartacus. "That sounds

like a Greek name. Are you from Greece, children?"

Francie looked at Bill and Nina hopelessly. How could they tell Spartacus where they were from? He'd never understand.

Spartacus bent forward. "You are escaped slaves, aren't you?" he whispered. "I have guessed your secret. And I know you will be killed if you are discovered. That is why I told my wife and the others to protect you. I admire you for daring to escape. I have talked about it for years, but I have never done it."

"Spartacus, we must talk to you. It's not exactly that we are escaped slaves," said Nina. She had decided that they were going to have to trust Spartacus with their secret.

Spartacus looked over at the guards. "It would be best if you pretended to be practicing with me," he said. "Take up a shield."

Nina lifted a small, round shield covered in leather. She was surprised at how heavy it was.

40

"Don't just let it hang from your wrist," insisted Spartacus. "Hold it in front of you."

Nina did as she was told. Luckily, she had been doing push-ups as part of her warm-up exercises, so her arms were strong. But even so, she kept wanting to lay down the shield.

"That's a good boy!" said Spartacus in a loud voice meant for the guards. Then he whispered, "All right, it's safe to talk now."

Nina didn't know where to begin. Finally

she just blurted out, "We're not from Greece. We're from the United States, which you don't even know about because it hasn't been discovered, and we don't know how we got here. Francie and I are girls, not boys. We were running with Bill this morning, two thousand years in the future. Now we're here, and we don't know how to get back home."

Spartacus dropped his wooden dagger and stared at her. "You are a girl?" he exclaimed.

Nina nodded.

"I've never seen a girl run so fast. This morning you ran as if you never got tired."

"That's because I run marathons," said Nina, annoyed. It bothered her that of all the amazing things she had told Spartacus, he seemed most surprised that she was a girl.

Spartacus turned to Francie. "You are a girl, too!" he whispered. "You run with the strength of a boy."

"I guess they haven't heard of women's lib yet," Francie whispered to Bill.

"Don't pick a fight with him, please,"

42

begged Bill in a whisper. "We need his help if we're going to survive. It's clear that he's the most popular gladiator around."

"Spartacus!" shouted one of the guards. "You spend too much time whispering with those children. You should be practicing."

"I'm glad you're so worried about me," Spartacus shouted back, not really meaning it.

"It's just that I've got a bet placed on you," laughed the guard.

"Do you really have to fight someone to the death on Saturday?" gasped Nina.

Spartacus shrugged. "I've survived thirty such fights so far. The Romans have been holding these contests for hundreds of years." Spartacus stared at Nina and Francie again. "I still can't believe you are girls. I will tell my wife and she will take you to the women's quarters. You can help her in the cookhouse."

"No!" shouted Nina, Francie, and Bill together. They shouted so loud that everything in the courtyard stopped.

"Spartacus!" called the guard. "What is

going on with those children? They are wasting your time."

"I am just teaching them some of the commands we gladiators use in the arena," Spartacus explained.

"*No* has never been a word a gladiator can use," yelled one of the guards. He laughed. "Whoever heard of a gladiator saying *no*?"

Spartacus gave the guard a dirty look and turned back to Nina, Francie, and Bill. "Don't shout, whatever you do. You will make the guards suspicious."

"But we don't want to be separated," cried Francie. "We have to stick together."

Spartacus looked at them with understanding. "You are the strangest girls I have ever met. But I will try to help you."

6

The Baths

"I'VE NEVER been so filthy in my life," complained Francie as she picked herself up out of the dirt. Each time she tried to swing the heavy wooden sword Spartacus had given her, she wound up off balance and in the dirt.

"Me too," said Nina. She was covered with dust. It was late afternoon, and Francie, Nina, and Bill had been trying to keep up with the well-trained gladiators all day. It was the hardest work they had ever done.

Suddenly, Marcus shouted out, "Get ready for the baths!"

"Hooray!" shouted Francie.

Britanicus smiled. "The baths are wonderful," he said. "We all go together. They are the best part of the day."

"Together!" shrieked Nina and Francie. They looked at each other in horror.

"Don't we get to take a bath by ourselves?" Francie asked.

"Whoever heard of taking a bath alone?" said Britanicus. "Besides, we all need a bath. Even your dog looks like he needs one."

Nina looked over at Fred. His coat was matted with dirt.

"Poor Fred," said Nina. "Can dogs go to the bath, too?"

"No," said Britanicus. "We can bathe him here. Only people go to the baths. Everyone goes—rich and poor, free and slave. It's fun. We gladiators are all in terrific shape. Some of the Romans look fat and ugly compared to us."

"You get to see everyone naked!" shrieked Francie.

"Of course," said Britanicus matter-of-factly.

Nina ran over to Spartacus. "We're sunk," she cried.

"Don't you know how to swim?" asked Spartacus. "Don't worry. The pool is not over your heads."

"No!" cried Nina, "we all know how to swim. But everyone will find out Francie and I are girls."

Spartacus's eyes twinkled, but he became serious when he realized how upset Nina was.

Spartacus called to his wife. "Two of these children must go with you," he said. "I will take the other with me."

"Spartacus, what are you talking about?" demanded Cipriana. "You are not making any sense."

Spartacus smiled. "These two are *girls*," he whispered, pointing to Nina and Francie. "And if I don't make sense, it is because these children make no sense. They say they are from a city called Denver, but they don't seem to know where it is."

"We know where it is," insisted Francie.

"It's just that we don't know how to get back there."

Spartacus's wife looked at them sadly. "All slaves talk that way about their homes. Come now. It's time for the baths."

Nina's mouth fell open when they stopped in front of a huge building with a rounded roof. "That's the bath?" she asked.

Cipriana smiled. "A bath to the Romans means more than just a chance to get clean. They have made bathing a high art. To tell you the truth, it's the only Roman custom I admire. Even the poorest citizen can come here and spend the day," she said, leading them inside.

Nina and Francie felt they had never seen a more beautiful building. The high, rounded ceiling was open to the light. The walls were marble and gold. And the floor was covered with brightly colored mosaics.

First Cipriana led them to a hot-water pool called the caladarium. The tile floors were heated from below by hot gases piped from outside the building.

"Ouch," shouted Francie as she dipped her toe into the pool. "It's too hot!"

"Just ease yourself in," said Cipriana. "You'll get used to it."

Slowly Nina and Francie lowered themselves into the water. Soon their muscles began to relax in the hot steam.

Francie stretched out her legs. She hadn't realized how tired she was.

"This is the life, isn't it?" Francie said to Nina.

"Not really," Nina replied. "Remember, we're still slaves."

"Aren't they worried that we'll escape from the bath?" Francie asked Cipriana.

Cipriana looked around to see if anyone was listening. "You must not talk of escape so loudly. I don't know where it was that you children escaped from, but it is very difficult to escape from here. If you were caught, you'd be put to death. Some masters will put a whole family to death just to teach the other slaves a lesson. Spartacus and I were captured after a battle in Thracia. We are lucky to have been kept together. Spartacus earns much money for our master, Lentulus Batiacus, and it is possible we will be able to buy our freedom someday."

Cipriana rose from the hot pool. "It's not good to stay in the hot pool too long," she warned. "Come with me to the tepidarium."

"What's that?" asked Nina.

"It's a slightly cooler room," said Cipriana. "It's my favorite."

The walls of the tepidarium were covered with paintings.

"Look! Isn't she beautiful?" cried Francie, pointing to a lovely picture of a young woman putting on her sandals.

"That's Venus," said Cipriana, "the goddess of love."

From the tepidarium Cipriana told them to dive into the frigidarium, a cold-water pool. This completed the process and left Francie and Nina feeling wide awake. They got their tunics back from the cloakroom and then wandered out to the garden.

Soon Spartacus and Bill and the other gladiators joined them. They all looked fresh and happy. "Wasn't that terrific?" said Bill.

Nina and Francie nodded. Several high-born young men were wrestling nearby. One pair jokingly asked Spartacus to join them. Spartacus shook his head.

"Everyone seems to like you so," said Nina. "They all know you."

"I wouldn't exactly say they like me," Spartacus said bitterly. "They cheer for me in the arena, but tomorrow they could have a new favorite. Then they would cheerfully turn thumbs down."

"What do you mean?" asked Francie worriedly.

"It means that I would be killed," Spartacus replied.

Francie shuddered. Nina and Bill stared at the ground. Suddenly all the good feeling from the baths seemed to drain away. To be a gladiator slave was a terrible fate. They had to find a way to escape back to the twentieth century. Otherwise, Nina, Francie, and Bill would most likely wind up dead on the arena floor, the fate of so many young gladiators before them.

ⴖⴖⴖⴖⴖⴖⴖⴖⴖⴖⴖⴖⴖⴖⴖⴖⴖⴖⴖⴖⴖ

Francie Gets Picked

THE NEXT day Britanicus decided to teach Francie how to use a sword. Francie had a bad habit of closing her eyes whenever Britanicus's wooden sword came close to her face.

Suddenly a hush fell over the yard. Francie's eyes were shut tight and she was swinging her wooden dagger wildly in the air when a voice she had never heard before said, "I admire that little one's spirit."

Francie turned around and opened her eyes. She found herself face to face with a boy about her own age. He was dressed in a snowy white tunic and he had a white toga wrapped around his shoulders. The toga had a deep purple band.

The boy's voice was high and whiny. "See Uncle," he shouted. "This one didn't stop fighting even when we entered the court-yard. I want this one to fight for my birthday." The boy grabbed Francie's arm and tried to push her in front of his uncle, a tall, heavy man who looked down at Francie as if she were a new horse he hadn't seen before.

"I don't remember buying this one," he said, turning to Marcus. The guard stood at attention, his whip always ready.

"I only noticed him myself yesterday, Lentulus Batiatus," said Marcus. "That one and two other children gave me some trouble on the morning run yesterday."

Lentulus Batiatus stared at Francie. "This one doesn't look very strong. I can't imagine why I would have bought him."

Francie got furious. The boy still had hold of her arm. She disliked the fact that Batiatus thought he owned her at all. She resented even *more* the fact that he didn't think her worth owning.

"I *am* strong!" shouted Francie. She violently pushed the young boy with her free arm. He was so surprised that she would dare touch him that he fell back and tripped over Britanicus's foot. The boy wound up in the mud.

"Look what the slave did to me," he said angrily.

"I was only showing your uncle that I was strong," said Francie.

"Shhh," whispered Britanicus. "It is best not to come to the attention of our owner, Lentulus Batiatus."

"Stop whispering, slaves," Batiatus shouted. He pointed to Francie. "Help my nephew Claudius out of the mud. You have done a good job of showing me how strong you are."

Something about his voice sounded threatening. Francie found herself wishing she had listened to Britanicus and kept her mouth shut. As she leaned over to help Claudius out of the mud, she caught sight of Nina and Bill standing with Spartacus in between them. Nina looked frightened, as if she knew something Francie didn't.

"You pushed me on purpose," said the boy. "You wanted me to fall in the mud."

"I did not," insisted Francie. "It was an accident. You were pinching my arm."

"Quiet, slave," ordered Batiatus. He turned to his nephew. "Come now, I told you that for your birthday you could pick two pairs of gladiators to fight in tomorrow's games. But we cannot take all day. Make your choice."

Claudius looked over the men and boys in front of him like a kid in a candy store with money to spend. He walked around pinching the muscled arms of different gladiators. He left Francie and Britanicus alone, and Francie took a deep breath of relief.

Claudius stopped in front of Nina, Spartacus, and Bill. Spartacus looked right through Claudius as if the boy were nothing more than a speck of dirt before his eyes.

"I want to see Spartacus fight for my birthday," piped the boy in his high voice.

"Of course," said Batiatus. "I'm not surprised. Spartacus is very popular with everyone these days."

Spartacus stood perfectly still. Nina felt far more respect for him than for Batiatus in his fine linen toga.

"Now, who shall I choose to fight Spartacus," said Claudius. He switched his glance to Bill. "Too skinny," he muttered.

He wandered up and down the rows of gladiators, trying to decide who should fight Spartacus. He came again to Francie, who was standing very quietly next to Britanicus.

"We know this one is strong," said Claudius with a laugh. "I want this one to fight Spartacus."

For a second Francie didn't realize he was talking about her. Then she felt her knees grow weak.

Batiatus laughed. "I do not think the crowds would enjoy the match," he said. "It would be over too soon. Pick another gladiator, my nephew—someone who will give the crowds a real fight."

"But I want to see this one fight," whined the boy. "You told me for my birthday I could pick any pair of gladiators I wanted."

Batiatus shook his head. "The pair must be evenly matched," he said. Batiatus looked over the courtyard filled with the men and boys he owned. He pointed to a tall blond man a foot taller than Spartacus.

"Why not choose Varnius to fight Spartacus. He is very good with the net." One of the favorite Roman sports was to have one man fight armed only with a net and a sharp spear and the other with just a short sword.

Claudius gave his uncle a sly look. "All right," Claudius said. "You can pair up Spartacus and Varnius, but that is *your* choice. I still get to pick *my* pair of gladiators to fight."

Claudius took a step forward and pointed to Francie and Britanicus.

"No!" shouted Nina so loudly that Batiatus turned around and stared at her.

Spartacus put his hand over Nina's mouth. "Do not say anything," he warned. "You will only make it worse and bring punishment on yourself."

Batiatus turned back to his nephew and Francie and Britanicus. He thought about them and then laughed out loud. "It is not a bad choice," he said. "The crowds may enjoy seeing two youngsters fight." Then he put his arm around his nephew's shoulders.

"Come," he said, "it is hot in the sunshine. We will go inside for refreshment." Batiatus turned to Marcus. "See that the two children are prepared to fight in the games tomorrow."

Their backs were turned so they did not see Francie slowly fall to the ground. Her last thought as she hit the ground was that tomorrow she would die and nothing could save her.

⊓⊔⊓⊔⊓⊔⊓⊔⊓⊔⊓⊔⊓⊔⊓⊔⊓⊔⊓⊔⊓⊔⊓⊔⊓⊔⊓⊔⊓⊔

8

Fight or Die

NINA AND Bill rushed over to Francie. Spartacus brought her some water. Soon Francie's eyes flickered open. She saw all her friends standing over her, looking worried. Fred was wagging his tail. For a second Francie forgot where she was and thought she was home in Denver. Even Spartacus just looked like a good friend of her parents' whom she especially liked.

But then she noticed the tunics and the hot Italian sun and she wanted to cry. "I'm going to be killed," she whispered in a shaky voice.

"I won't kill you," said Britanicus. "They

can't make me." He looked over at Spartacus. "What can I do?" he wailed, nearly in
tears. "I don't want to fight with Francie.
Francie is my friend."

"All gladiators must kill their friends,"
said Spartacus bitterly. "That is the Roman
way."

Nina put her arms around Francie.
Francie's head was resting in her lap.
"Francie is not going to fight," she said. "I'm
much stronger. I'll fight."

"No," said Bill. "I'll go instead of Francie.
Britanicus and I are about the same size. At
least it will be an even match."

"None of you children will fight," said
Spartacus. "It is bad enough that the Romans send men to their deaths. They must
not be permitted to send children."

"I want to go home to Denver," bawled
Francie.

Spartacus patted her on the head. "Don't
cry, little one. We will find some way to get
you home and out of this."

Francie looked up at him through her

tears. "But you don't even know where Denver is," she cried.

Spartacus laughed gently. "No, but I know how much all slaves want to return to their homes." He helped Francie to her feet.

Just then Cipriana hurried out to the courtyard. "I heard a rumor that one of the children is being forced to fight," she said, running to Nina.

"It's not me. It's Francie," Nina explained.

"This can't be allowed to happen," said Cipriana. "I would rather die myself than have to watch these children fight."

Several of the gladiators had broken into small groups, and now they were whispering among themselves. The guards circled the courtyard nervously. They knew that something out of the ordinary was going on.

Spartacus gathered the gladiators around him. "I agree with my wife. The children must not fight. But perhaps it is time for all of us to stop fighting just to amuse the Romans."

"But if we don't fight, they will kill us anyway," said one of the gladiators. "They will call us cowards and slaughter us like animals in the arena."

"So instead, we slaughter each other," answered Spartacus. "Wouldn't it be better to die fighting for our freedom, than to die just to bring a little excitement to the crowds."

"Right!" shouted Nina, so loud that the guards heard her.

"Hey!" called Marcus. "What are you slaves doing? You should be practicing for the games."

"We are," said Spartacus. "We are teaching the children so you will have a good fight to watch tomorrow."

Marcus looked disgusted. "I don't like the idea of watching children fight," he said.

Even though he often used the whip, Marcus could be a fair man, and Spartacus knew it. Spartacus looked Marcus straight in the eye and said, "Leave us alone for a minute."

Marcus looked confused, as if he didn't quite know what to do. He glanced at Francie, who looked terrified. Nina was holding her hand, and Bill had his arm around her shoulders. Britanicus stood sadly to the side.

"You can speak among yourselves for just a moment," said Marcus. He spun on his heels, motioning the other guards to leave the gladiators alone.

The tension in the courtyard seemed thicker than the fog that had surrounded Nina, Francie, and Bill and brought them to this strange place. They looked around at the gladiators. They might be slaves, but most of them were the best fighters in the Roman Republic.

"Batiatus has gone too far this time," said Spartacus. He didn't shout, but his voice carried clearly. Marcus stood with his back to the gladiators, pretending not to hear.

"We have all dreamed of escape. Now is the time to stop dreaming. It is time for us to fight for ourselves, for our freedom."

Varnius stepped forward with one of the wooden practice swords. He waved it in the air. "What good will these toys do against the Romans' sharp swords?" he asked. "Our fight will be over in minutes. We will never get out of the courtyard alive."

Several gladiators nodded in agreement. "Right," shouted one. "We only have wooden play swords. It's hopeless."

"Wait!" said Spartacus. "It's not hopeless. Our lives are hopeless right now. We all know we will die in the arena sooner or later."

"But some of us might live to buy our freedom," said Varnius. "If we try to escape, we all die."

Spartacus looked from one face to the next.

"I'll fight with you, Spartacus," said Nina. "We have nothing to lose."

"Me, too," shouted Francie and Bill together.

"The children are brave," said Spartacus. "Shouldn't we be as brave?"

"The children don't know any better," muttered one gladiator.

"I agree," said Spartacus. "It would be foolish to fight with only wooden weapons. But what if we wait until tomorrow when we are at the arena. There, we are always given real weapons because the Romans like to see real blood."

"Now that's a good idea," said Varnius. "I'm willing to join you as long as I have a fighting chance."

"Me, too," shouted one of the other gladiators.

"Count me in," said another.

"Wait a minute, Spartacus," said Cipriana. "In our kitchens we have many things that could be used for weapons—all sorts of knives and heavy cooking tools. Even our bronze frying pans could be used to hit someone over the head."

Francie started to giggle at the idea of hitting Roman soldiers over the head with a frying pan.

"Shhh," said Spartacus. "Cipriana is right. If we go to the arena with some weapons hidden, we will be in a much better position to try our escape. In the morning, Cipriana and the other women will try to slip us anything from the kitchen that will help. There is always so much confusion the mornings we go to the arena. It should be easy to hide our weapons."

"Wait a minute," said Bill, who felt that things were moving too fast for him. "Where are we going to escape to?"

"We will try to get over the mountains and back to our homes," said Spartacus. "Perhaps the Romans will get tired of chasing us. But we will face that problem when we get free."

Bill felt a cold fear in the pit of his stomach. The chances of the gladiators escaping appeared very slim. Spartacus seemed to sense his mood.

"We have no choice," he said grimly. "If we do nothing, your friend will die in the arena." He glanced down fondly at Francie. "She is a very brave girl, but she could not survive in the arena for more than a minute against Britanicus."

"Well, maybe I could survive a minute," said Francie gamely.

9

└┌┐┌┐┌┐┌┐┌┐┌┐┌┐┌┐┌┐┌┐┌┐┌┐┌┐┌┐┘

Hidden Weapons

NINA'S EYES snapped open. In the dim light she made out the sleeping forms of Bill and Francie on the floor. Instantly she knew where she was. And somehow that seemed more scary than anything that had happened before. It was as if she no longer expected to wake up home in Denver.

She choked back a sob. She didn't want to wake up Francie and Bill. At least Cipriana had arranged for them all to sleep in the same room, and even for Fred to be allowed to stay with them. Fred seemed to sense that Nina was awake. He snuggled closer, as if trying to comfort her.

Nina stared at the small square of light coming in from the high window. She patted Fred's side. He wagged his tail. Nina wondered whether Fred realized they had traveled back in time. What would happen to Fred if they were killed? Would somebody take care of him? Would he ever find his way back to the twentieth century?

Nina shivered. She wished she could stop thinking about dying, but it seemed so unlikely that they would live through the day. "If we die, will our parents ever find out?" she wondered. And with that thought, she started to cry.

Bill heard her and woke up. "Nina," he whispered, "are you all right?"

Nina shook her head no, and tried to stop the tears. "I was just thinking that we'll probably be killed today, and I started to cry."

"Gee, Nina," said Francie, trying to make her friend laugh, "I can't imagine crying over a little thing like that."

Nina managed a weak smile. Francie

hugged her. "As long as we stick together, maybe we'll be all right."

"I know," said Nina. "Besides I'd much rather try to escape than go into that arena."

"Me too," said Francie. "Especially since I was the first one picked."

Suddenly there was a knock at the door. Cipriana whispered, "Are you awake?"

Francie let her in. Cipriana's face, normally dark and tanned, looked almost ghostlike. "Are you children ready?" she asked.

"Is Spartacus really going ahead with his plan to escape?" asked Bill.

Cipriana nodded her head. "We talked about it all night and decided we had to take the chance. We couldn't let them put you in the arena."

Francie felt a sick feeling in the pit of her stomach. "I don't want everybody to get hurt because of me," she said. "You could hide me somewhere so I wouldn't have to fight Britanicus. Then Spartacus, you, and the others wouldn't have to go through all this."

Cipriana shook her head and smiled. "You must not imagine that everyone is doing this just for you," she said. "It is true that Spartacus was furious when you were picked to fight in the arena. But we have been dreaming of trying to escape ever since we were captured."

Francie blushed. "I didn't mean that everyone was doing it for me. I just . . . just . . ." she stammered.

"Do not think about it any more," said Cipriana. "You must come to breakfast. I have to get back to the cookhouse now. The other women and I have been thinking of ways to sneak weapons out of the kitchen. We will succeed."

At breakfast all the gladiators and the female slaves acted as if nothing unusual was happening. Marcus and the other guards stood around looking bored.

"Cipriana," shouted Spartacus, "since I have to fight today I need more food. Please give me an extra dollop of honey."

"I will have to bring the big pot," said

Cipriana. "There is only a little left in the bottom. You can scrape it out."

Cipriana brought out a huge honey pot. She carried it high, as if it were light. But as she passed, Nina noticed that the muscles in Cipriana's arms were tight. Beads of sweat had broken out on Cipriana's forehead.

Cipriana put the honey pot down next to Spartacus. "There is only a little left at the bottom," she said. "You will have to dig for it yourself."

Spartacus reached deep into the honey pot. Cipriana moved so that her body blocked the guards' view of her husband.

Nina saw Spartacus take several knives and heavy items out of the honey pot and hide them in his lap. When Cipriana returned to the kitchen carrying the pot, her muscles no longer strained.

Britanicus, who was sitting next to Nina, elbowed her in the ribs. "Look what I got," he whispered. Nina looked down. A large metal spit from the fire was lying across his lap.

"How are you going to carry that out of here?" whispered Nina.

Britanicus looked around. "I don't know. I just stole it. It will make a wonderful weapon."

"If you can hide it until you need it," warned Nina. She leaned over and told Bill what Britanicus was hiding.

"Maybe if we each walk on either side of Britanicus the guards won't notice," Bill whispered. "I'll tell Francie."

"Are you children ready for today?" shouted Marcus, stopping them in the court-yard.

"We're as ready as we're going to be," said Francie truthfully.

Britanicus shifted his weight, trying to keep the heavy metal bar from Marcus's eyes.

"I want to wish you both good luck," said Marcus.

"Thank you," replied Francie quickly, worried that Marcus would spot Britanicus's weapon. The children did a kind of sideways shuffle until they were out of sight. Then they all breathed more freely.

10

We Who Are About to Die Salute You

"It's SPOOKY down here," whispered Nina. They were walking through a stone passageway underneath the arena. Suddenly they heard a loud roar.

"What was that noise?" demanded Francie.

"A lion," said Britanicus matter-of-factly.

"A lion?" yelled Francie. "What's a lion doing here?"

"In between gladiator contests, they send out captured criminals and let the lions eat them," Britanicus said.

"You mean there are people-eating lions loose down here," said Francie.

"They aren't loose," explained Britanicus. "They are in the animal room. But if Spartacus's plan works, we will have to go near them because the weapons for the gladiators are stored next to the animals."

"Terrific," said Francie. "I have some choices. Either I try to fight you in the arena, or I get eaten by a lion."

"Or we fight for our freedom," reminded Nina.

Just then a man who looked at least ten feet tall came down the passageway. His head nearly touched the ceiling.

"What's *that*?" shouted Bill. "A giant!"

Britanicus laughed. "It's just one of the acrobats on stilts. He's practicing. Before the gladiators go on, the clowns perform for the crowds."

"It's just like a circus," said Francie, "only people die."

"Our word *circus* comes from the Roman games," said Nina.

"I may never go to a circus again," said Francie.

Spartacus looked very serious. "You children must listen carefully. Soon the guards will allow us into the weapons room to choose the ones we want for the afternoon. Francie, if you are brave enough you could help us."

"How?" asked Francie, a little worried.

"The guards know that you are not used to the arena," said Spartacus. "You should take a long time choosing your weapon. Try each one, then hand it to a waiting gladiator. Act as if you are not sure which one you want to use. Then, when I give the signal, run behind me. As soon as the escape begins, find Cipriana, for she will know where to go. Do you have the nerve to put on a show in front of the guards?"

Francie nodded her head. "I'll do it," she said softly.

"Nina and I will be right by your side," Bill promised.

Francie gulped. "But you won't be the one who has to fool the guards," she said.

Lentulus Batiatus and his nephew Claudius were waiting for them in the weapons room. It was getting hard to hear. Already people were pouring into the amphitheater, shouting greetings to each other. It sounded just like a crowd getting ready to see the Superbowl.

Lentulus Batiatus grabbed Francie by the arm and pushed her toward his nephew.

"Claudius wants to wish you luck," he said.

Claudius sneered at Francie. "You are very lucky," he said. "Most gladiators do not get to go into the arena so young."

"Some luck," mumbled Francie.

"What is that?" demanded Batiatus.

"Nothing," said Francie, keeping her eyes on the ground.

"Uncle," piped Claudius in his high voice, "make this rude gladiator give me the gladiator's salute now. I may not be able to hear it in the arena."

"It's against tradition," said Batiatus. "It might be bad luck."

"Oh please, Uncle," begged Claudius. Nina watched him with hatred. She wondered what the gladiator's salute was. And she worried about what would happen when they found out Francie didn't know it either.

Francie felt exactly like a trapped animal.

"Please Uncle," begged Claudius. "Make this gladiator salute me. It's my birthday. I'm sure it won't bring bad luck."

"All right," said Batiatus, letting out a long sigh. He pointed to Francie. "Give my nephew the salute," he said in a weary voice.

Francie was in a panic. She didn't have the slightest idea of what she was supposed to do.

"Wait!" shouted a voice from the back. It was Spartacus. "Gladiators must not give the salute without a weapon. It is against the custom. This young gladiator must choose a weapon first."

Batiatus nodded his head. "I suppose you're right." He turned to Francie. "Pick your weapon," he said, "but be quick about it. The crowds are getting restless, and you and Britanicus will be on first."

Batiatus stepped aside so Francie could choose from the weapons hanging on the

wall. Francie went up and lifted down a heavy sword.

"This one is good," she said.

"Fine," said Batiatus. "It is yours."

"But it's a little heavy." Francie handed it to Spartacus who had worked his way up from the back of the room. "Hold it for me please," said Francie. "I *may* want to use it." Spartacus took the sword.

Then Francie pulled down a Thracian dagger. Its cutting edge was as sharp as a razor. "This feels good," she said, "but it's a little light." She handed the dagger to Varnius.

One by one, Francie pulled down the weapons from the wall and pretended to test each one before deciding it just wasn't right.

"Make up your mind," said Batiatus impatiently. "Soon you will have tried every weapon in the room."

"Well, I always say you can't be too careful about your weapons," said Francie. She glanced around. Almost every gladiator in the room was armed.

"Now!" shouted Spartacus with a roar. Francie ducked as Spartacus swung his sword high in the air. All the gladiators leaped forward.

Nina and Bill grabbed Francie's hands and rushed to the back of the room, trying desperately to find Cipriana. The guards cried out as they realized what was happening. Soon the room was filled with the sound of metal crashing on metal.

Britanicus ran beside them, using the heavy metal spit from the cookfire like a battering ram.

"Over here!" shouted Cipriana. She gathered the children around her. Several gladiators fought off the guards with the weapons Francie had given them. Others used the kitchen knives to good advantage.

Before more guards could be called, the gladiators had battled their way through the passageways under the arena, out into the streets.

"Quick!" shouted Spartacus. "We must get through the city gates before the guards close them."

As they ran, Francie tugged on Spartacus's tunic. "I have just one question," she said out of breath. "What was the salute I was supposed to give?"

Spartacus smiled. "If we are successful, no gladiator will ever have to give it again," he said. "I have always hated saying it."

"But what is it?" insisted Francie.

" 'We who are about to die salute you,' " said Spartacus grimly.

11

A Lucky Break

As THE gladiators ran through the streets, many slaves realized what was happening and joined them. Francie found herself shouting. "Come with us!"

"Francie," yelled Nina. "We aren't free yet. Let's just get out of the city alive."

"That's not going to be easy," said Bill. "Look ahead."

At the city gates, a small group of Roman soldiers had realized the slaves were trying to escape. They lined themselves up in front of the gate.

Spartacus held up his hand, warning the

gladiators and the other escaped slaves to
stop. "We will have to fight our way through
the city gates," he said. "Quickly, divide
yourselves into four groups."

"Won't we be stronger if we stay together?" asked Varnius.

"No," said Spartacus. "Trust me."

"Let's make sure we stay in the same group," Nina whispered. Francie and Bill nodded their heads.

"Where's Fred?" shouted Francie.

"He's right here," said Cipriana. "Ever

since I started feeding him, he's been sticking to my side."

Spartacus came over to Cipriana. "Stay with the children," he said.

"No," said Cipriana, holding up a kitchen knife in her hand. "I will fight for my freedom."

"We will fight, too," said Nina.

Spartacus nodded grimly.

Quickly the gladiators formed four columns and advanced toward the Roman soldiers.

The soldiers couldn't decide which group to attack first. With the soldiers divided, Spartacus gave another command, and the gladiators quickly closed ranks, completely surrounding the Roman soldiers.

Nina, Francie, and Bill raised their weapons and shouted, but it was hard for them to see what was happening. The gladiators were used to fighting, and they battled the Romans fiercely. The struggle was over in minutes. Only a few soldiers escaped the gladiators' swords, fleeing through the streets.

With a shout of victory, Spartacus led the gladiators out the gates. Nina, Francie, and Bill rushed through, holding hands.

"We are free!" shouted Britanicus, as they gathered in a field outside the city gates. Everywhere Nina, Francie, and Bill looked, gladiators and slaves were hugging each other, overjoyed at their victory.

Only Spartacus looked worried. "We are not free yet," he warned. "They will be sending troops after us. Many of you who have just joined us are house slaves. We need time to teach you how to fight. I suggest we climb that mountain. We need more weapons, too. But for now we must escape to the safety of the mountains. It is our only chance.

Off the road in the distance they could see high hills. Towering above the hills was a mountain. Spartacus pointed to it and said, "From the high ground we will be able to spot the troops from Rome. We will be able to hide there until we are ready to fight."

Francie looked up at the mountain. "It's awfully high," she said, thinking about the tiring climb up there.

"It's Mount Vesuvius," Britanicus explained.

"Mount Vesuvius!" cried Bill. "That's a volcano. That's the mountain that buried Pompeii."

"Don't be silly," said Britanicus. "Pompeii is an even bigger city than Capua."

Bill shook his head. "I guess Mount Vesuvius hasn't erupted yet."

"Let's hope it doesn't happen when we're on it," said Francie.

Britanicus looked at them as if they were crazy.

Just then Fred began barking furiously at a cart coming down the road. He took off after it.

"Fred! Come back here!" shouted Nina, running after him.

As the cart got closer, the reason for Fred's excitement became clear. Another English sheep dog was riding in the cart.

Nina reached the cart just as Fred was about to jump in. Both dogs were wagging their tails as if they were long lost friends.

"You must be a slave from Britain, too," the old man who was driving the cart said to Nina. "My old dog is all I have left from the days when I was a free man."

"We are not slaves any more," said Nina excitedly. "We are free. We have all just escaped." Nina pointed to the group of gladiators and slaves.

Britanicus, Bill, and Francie came running up to Nina. "Hurry, Nina," shouted Francie. "Spartacus wants us all to start for the mountain."

Nina turned to the old man. "Come with us," she pleaded. "It is your chance to be free."

The old man began to laugh gleefully. Nina looked puzzled.

"Why is he laughing?" she asked Britanicus. "Did I say something funny?"

Britanicus shrugged his shoulders. "Many people from my country have a strange sense of humor," he said. "But I don't know why this old man is laughing so hard."

The old man wiped the tears from his eyes. "Tell me, children," he said. "Who is your leader in this escape?"

"I am," said Spartacus, walking up to the cart. "Will you join us? All slaves are welcome."

"Gladly," said the old man. "But you don't realize how lucky you are. Just look in my cart."

Spartacus lifted the cloth covering the back of the cart. The cart was loaded to the top with weapons.

"What in the world . . . ?" Spartacus exclaimed.

"The gods must be smiling on you," said the old man. "I was supposed to deliver these weapons to Rome. I'd rather they be used to fight for freedom." The old man laughed again. "My master will never know what happened to me. I have been looking for the courage to rebel ever since I was captured. Now, I will die a free man. Here, take the weapons. But leave one sharp sword for me."

12

A Desperate Trick

THEY HAD gone only about a mile when Spartacus spotted soldiers from Capua pouring out of the city gates, coming after them. "I had hoped we would have more time to get away," he muttered.

"They're gaining," Nina whispered. Spartacus had kept them moving as fast as possible, but the soldiers were able to march at double time. Even though the gladiators and slaves had a head start, the Roman soldiers were moving closer.

"We're going to have to fight them sometime," warned Cipriana.

"I had hoped we would reach the mountain before nightfall," said Spartacus.

"We can fight and win!" the old man shouted, waving his sword in the air.

Spartacus smiled. "We can fight them, but we cannot hope to win. At least not yet. They outnumber us." Spartacus looked back at the Roman army in the distance. Closer by, Fred and the other English sheep dog were chasing a herd of cattle.

Suddenly Spartacus began to grin. Then he started to laugh. Nina, Francie, Bill, and even Cipriana looked at him as if he were crazy.

"Britanicus," said Spartacus excitedly. "Didn't you herd cattle when you were a small boy?"

"Yes," said Britanicus seriously. "But now I am a soldier, willing to die for freedom."

Spartacus shook his head. "It is more important that you herd cattle. If you can bring those cattle to me, we may be able to save our lives. If not, we may all be dead by nightfall."

"Are you crazy, Spartacus?" demanded

Cipriana. "The Romans will be upon us within the hour. We must think up a way to fight them."

"I'd rather fool them," said Spartacus.

Cipriana and the gladiators looked at him as if he had gone mad.

"We mustn't waste time," said Spartacus urgently. "Trust me. I have a plan."

"I'll go help get the cows," said Nina. "Fred is already over there."

"Me, too," Francie and Bill volunteered.

"Good," said Spartacus. "Only hurry."

Nina, Francie, Bill, and Britanicus ran through the pasture after the cattle.

"What do you think Spartacus has in mind?" Francie asked.

"I don't know," said Bill. "But it had better work. Otherwise the Romans will win. We can't fight that many of them."

As they got closer to the cattle, Britanicus warned them to slow down. "Do you see the one with hay on its horns," he whispered.

"Yes," Bill replied. "It looks like the hay was tied on. How strange!"

"We have to be careful of that one," said Britanicus. "The Romans tie hay around the horns of the dangerous bulls so that the people who meet them will be on guard."

"Maybe we should leave them all alone," Francie suggested. She was amazed to see how big the cattle looked close up. She and her friends had grown up in the city. The closest they had ever gotten to a cow was on a fifth-grade school trip to a ranch.

"We have to get behind them," said Britanicus. "It's important not to scare them. You just sort of cluck at them."

"Cluck?" asked Francie. "Are you sure you're not talking about chickens?"

But Britanicus had snuck behind the cattle and was making deep clucking noises in the back of his throat. The cattle seemed to understand. They moved slowly toward a clump of pine trees where Spartacus was waiting with a large group.

"Good!" cried Spartacus when they reached him. "I see that one has hay on its horns already."

"What do you mean, 'good'?" demanded Bill. "That one is dangerous."

"We have to tie hay onto all their horns," said Spartacus. "Quickly!"

"What?" exclaimed Cipriana.

"We're going to use Hannibal's trick," explained Spartacus. "Hannibal was a general of one of Rome's enemies, and he brought Rome to its knees. That was over a hundred years ago. Once when Hannibal was outnumbered by the Romans, he tied hay to the tips of a large herd of cattle. When he lit the hay, it looked just like torches held by soldiers. In the dark, the Romans thought Hannibal had twice the number of troops that he actually had, and they followed the

cattle. If the trick worked for Hannibal, it might work for us. But we must work fast. It is nearly dark, and the Romans will be upon us soon."

Spartacus and the other gladiators had gathered small piles of hay. They tied the hay to the horns of the cattle.

"Now we won't be able to tell which one is the dangerous bull," Nina whispered to Britanicus.

"I hope some Roman finds out the hard way," Britanicus answered.

The sky was dark now. In the distance, the Roman torches shone brightly as the soldiers moved closer. "The Romans don't like to fight at night," said Spartacus. "But they will not want to allow slaves another day of freedom. They will attack us even though it is getting dark. Quick! We must light the torches."

Spartacus lit the hay on the tip of the cattle's long horns. The other gladiators soon helped him light the torches.

"Now what?" whispered Nina.

"Quickly, before the cattle grow restless, we must get them moving in the right direction," said Spartacus. Then he waved at the cattle, but they ignored him.

"I can tell you haven't spent much time around cows," said Britanicus.

"I have always been a soldier," said Spartacus, sounding short-tempered. "Perhaps now is the time to show off *your* skills, Britanicus. Do not waste more time. Get them moving!"

Britanicus clucked at the cattle as he walked behind them slowly. Immediately the cows headed in the right direction.

"What's the difference between my wave, and his clucking sound?" asked Spartacus, puzzled.

"I don't know," said Francie. "But the cattle seem to understand Britanicus."

"Thank goodness," sighed Spartacus.

As the cattle began to spread out on their way down the hill, they also moved faster and faster—until they were almost stampeding out of sight.

"That's just what we need!" Spartacus shouted.

In the dark, the torches on the cattle's horns shone brightly as they ran down the hill.

"If ever we need luck, we need it now!" cried Spartacus.

"I'll cross my fingers," said Francie.

A sudden hush fell over Spartacus and the rest as they peered into the darkness. The Roman troops were so close that Nina, Francie, and Bill could hear their heavy footsteps, marching together.

Then suddenly, the footsteps stopped.

"They have seen the torches!" whispered Spartacus. "They must be deciding what to do. If they come any closer toward us, we are doomed."

Francie closed her eyes. She couldn't bear to look.

"What's happening?" Francie whispered in a scared voice.

"I can't tell," whispered Bill.

Spartacus cursed under his breath. "They

101

are just standing still. Wait! Now they are
starting to move."

"But in what direction?" whispered
Francie urgently.

"Towards the cows!" cried Bill.

"Shh," warned Spartacus, but his voice
sounded full of joy.

"Is it true?" whispered Francie, finally
daring to open her eyes.

"Yes, look!" whispered Spartacus. They
think the cows are us. They are following

the cows!" He began to laugh. "We tricked
them. They think we are trying to run away.
They will follow the cattle until the torches
burn out. We have a chance now to climb the
mountain to safety.

"If our luck holds," said Cipriana, "we
may all live to see our homes again."

"Home!" whispered Nina to Francie and
Bill. "Even if we're free, I don't think we'll
ever see home again."

⊓⊓⊓⊓⊓⊓⊓⊓⊓⊓⊓⊓⊓⊓⊓⊓⊓⊓⊓⊓⊓⊓⊓⊓⊓⊓⊓

13

Trapped

"WE WILL not sleep tonight," said Britanicus. They had begun the long climb up the slopes of Mount Vesuvius under the cover of darkness. There was only one path up the mountain. The far side of Mount Vesuvius was one sheer high cliff.

"The Romans will never find us here," said Francie when they finally neared the top. It was overgrown with thick vines.

Spartacus shook his head sadly. "It won't be that easy. We have gained time, but the Romans will come after us again. We must begin training right away for battle."

"Spartacus," complained Varnius. "We

have to rest sometime. Surely, we are safe up here for a little while. Let us sleep."

Many of the other gladiators shouted their agreement.

"All right," said Spartacus. "We will rest, but tomorrow we begin training."

The next day Spartacus gathered together all the gladiators and escaped slaves.

"The Romans will have already discovered the trick with the cattle. They will guess we are hiding here. We must teach you how to fight. I am asking each gladiator to work with a small group of slaves. It is our only hope."

Spartacus began to divide up the newly escaped slaves.

"What about the women?" said Cipriana. "We must be taught to fight, too."

"And the children," said Nina. "We can help."

"You'll need everyone who can lift a sword," said Francie.

"You are right," said Spartacus. "I, myself, will teach the women. Britanicus, you will be in charge of the children. Nina, Francie, and Bill will help you."

There were over twenty children to work with. "I suggest we start with a run," said Nina.

"Nina will use any excuse to run," whispered Francie.

"It's a good idea," said Britanicus. "That is how we got strong as gladiators. Our masters made us run every day. Now we can run for freedom."

"At least it's better than claiming we're running for fun," muttered Francie as they started out.

"The Romans! The Romans!" cried one of the sentinels that Spartacus had posted. Nina, Francie, and Bill ran to a lookout point. Francie got there first and gasped.

A huge army of more than three thousand soldiers had suddenly appeared in the field below, blocking off the only escape down Mount Vesuvius.

"They found us!" shrieked Francie, shocked at the size of the Roman army.

"We'll never make it off this mountain alive. If only we had time to train."

"Shhh," said Nina impatiently. "You don't want to scare the little kids."

Bill poked Nina in the ribs. "Look," he whispered. Spartacus was huddled with Cipriana, Varnius, and several other of the original gladiators. They all looked extremely worried.

"Are we going to die?" whimpered one little boy who had recently joined them.

"No," said Nina. "You must trust Spartacus. "Besides, we are teaching you to fight so that you can beat the Romans."

"I wish I believed that," whispered Britanicus fearfully. "I agree with Francie. I don't think any of us will make it off this mountain alive."

Just then Spartacus walked by.

"Where are you going?" asked Nina.

"I want to look at the far side of the mountain again. Perhaps there is a way down the cliffs after all. We are safe for the moment. The Romans won't come after us.

They would rather starve us up here. They know our gladiators are good fighters, and they want to avoid a battle if they can."

As Spartacus headed down the path, Fred ran after him. Spartacus patted the dog on the head. Fred wagged his tail and then bounded up ahead.

"Fred!" shouted Nina.

"It's all right," said Spartacus. "I'll look after him."

"Can we come look at the cliffs, too?" asked Francie.

"I suppose so," said Spartacus. "Perhaps, you will spot something I might miss."

As they walked through the thick vines, Francie asked, "Is there any hope?" She thought of the huge army camped below.

"There is always hope," said Spartacus.

"I think we can win, don't you?" said Bill. He was trying to sound brave, but his voice came out sounding scared.

"It would be certain death to try to fight the Romans now," Spartacus said bluntly. "I have only a few good fighters. Our only hope is to find another way off this mountain and surprise the Romans. Then, perhaps we can gain enough time to make our way to the Alps, and then to our homes."

As he was talking, Spartacus had grabbed one of the many wild vines that grew along the top of the mountain. It was extremely strong. Spartacus held the vine in his hand while they walked. They reached the far edge of the cliffs, and Spartacus paused before a crack in the rock. He seemed to be lost in thought. He dangled the vine over the cliff.

Fred started to play with the loose end of the vine. Suddenly his paw slipped. He tried to save himself, scrambling for a foothold on the cliff.

"Oh no!" cried Nina, making a grab for Fred. But he slipped out of her grasp. "*Fred!*" shouted Nina. She flung herself on her stomach to try to see over the cliff.

"Be careful!" shouted Spartacus.

"Fred!" sobbed Nina. "He's dead."

Suddenly they heard a high-pitched

bark coming from below them on the cliff.

"He's alive!" cried Francie. "He must be on a ledge."

"I've got to go get him," said Nina. She started to ease herself over the cliff.

"Wait!" commanded Spartacus. "You'll get hurt. But the vines. I can make a ladder out of them." Spartacus took out a knife that he wore around his waist and cut several vines, tying them together to form a strong ladder.

He threw it over the cliff. "Hold it," he called. "I'll go down and get the dog."

"Wait!" said Nina. "I'm much lighter, and I'm a good climber. It will be better if I try it. And Fred knows me. He won't panic." Spartacus hesitated, but he had to admit that Nina's idea made sense.

Spartacus tied the vine to a tree, and held it tight while Nina started to climb down. The ladder stretched nearly fifty feet to a plateau. Nina looked down. A thick fog was coming up the mountain.

Fred came running up to her. "He's fine! Fred's all right!" shouted Nina. But as she shouted, Fred bounded across the plateau away from her. The cliff was much less steep here, and Fred scrambled down the mountain.

"Oh no!" shouted Nina. "Fred, come back."

Francie and Bill stood at the top of the cliff, looking down and trying to catch sight of Nina. "I think we should go down and help her catch Fred," said Francie. Bill nodded.

"All right," said Spartacus. "Go down the ladder carefully." He had a smile on his face. "In fact, once you get back up here with Fred, I think I owe that dog a big thank you. He may have shown us a way out of here."

Francie and Bill stepped down the vine ladder. They could see the fog creeping up the mountain. When they reached the plateau, the fog was so thick they could no longer see Spartacus at the top of the cliff. In the distance they could hear Fred barking and Nina shouting at him to come back.

"We'd better follow her voice," said Francie.

"This fog is strange," said Bill. Suddenly, he turned to Francie in shock. But he couldn't see her through the fog.

⊓⊔⊓⊔⊓⊔⊓⊔⊓⊔⊓⊔⊓⊔⊓⊔⊓⊔⊓⊔⊓⊔⊓⊔⊓⊔⊓⊔

Out of Time

THE AIR was cooler. Nina felt the change first. Instantly she knew what had happened. She stared at the black asphalt road beneath her feet. The side of the road was lined with Aspen trees. Fred stood next to her, wagging his tail happily. Then she saw Bill and Francie walking out of the fog. They both looked very pale. They were dressed in their shorts and tops again.

"Where is Spartacus?" shouted Francie.

"We're back home," said Bill in a shocked voice.

"But Spartacus needs us," Francie wailed.

"Were we dreaming?" asked Nina.

Francie and Bill shook their heads. "It couldn't have been a dream. The three of us wouldn't have had the same one," insisted Bill.

Slowly they walked back down the road, too stunned to talk. They reached Nina's house first.

Her parents were just about to go for their morning run.

"Hi," said Nina's mother. "Did you have a good run?"

Nina stared at her. "Didn't you miss us?" she asked.

"Why we just assumed you were out for a run," answered her mother.

"What day is it?" asked Francie.

Nina's mother looked at her strangely. "Saturday, Francie. Are you all right?"

Francie nodded her head dumbly.

"We're fine . . . Mom . . . fine," said Nina in a shaky voice.

Nina's mother shrugged her shoulders, kissed her daughter lightly, and then went out the door for her run.

Bill sank down on the couch. "I don't believe it," he said. "No time in the twentieth century went by."

"How could that have happened?" Francie wondered.

"We must have somehow traveled beyond the speed of light," said Nina, "and . . ."

"But that's impossible," said Francie.

"It's as if we were on some kind of time warp," said Bill. "Maybe it was because we're young and were running hard."

"Who's going to believe us?" asked Francie. "They'll think we're making it up."

"I don't think we should tell anybody," said Nina seriously.

"But . . . someone should know," Francie protested.

"No. I agree with Nina," said Bill. "Something very special happened to us. I think we should keep it a secret—at least until we know more about it."

"Let's make a pact," said Nina. She looked at Francie intently. "Do you, Francie, swear never to tell anyone that we traveled in time?"

"I swear," said Francie softly.

"I swear also," said Bill. "But what happened to Spartacus? I wonder if he ever escaped the Romans."

"Wait a minute," said Nina, "I'll go look it up." She went to the encyclopedia. As she read, the color drained from her face. "You won't believe this," she said.

Nina started to read out loud:

Spartacus led a revolt of the slaves against their Roman masters from 73 B.C. to 71 B.C. He was a gladiator owned by Lentulus Batiatus who had a training school for gladiators in Capua. Batiatus was a very cruel man, and seventy-eight gladiators escaped armed with knives and other utensils stolen from the cookhouse.

On the road outside Capua, they captured a cart filled with weapons for gladiators in Rome. They defeated the soldiers sent out for them from Capua. Then they hid in the crater of Vesuvius. An army from Rome blocked the only known path down the mountain, but Spartacus and his men escaped by tying thick vines together and scaling a steep cliff.

"He escaped!" shouted Francie with joy.

Nina patted Fred on the head. "You showed him the way, boy. If you hadn't fallen down the cliff, he might never have discovered how to get down the ladder."

"But if it's true," said Bill, "then we had to·

have been there . . . somehow. We *were* there."

"I know," said Nina. "It's the strangest thing. It's almost as if we *needed* to be there."

"I wonder if we'll ever be able to go back in time again," said Francie.

"I don't know," said Nina, "but we can't stop running. We'll just have to run every day the way we always do, and then . . . ."

"Where are we going to run tomorrow?" asked Bill.

"And when?" asked Francie.

About the Story

THE DETAILS of Roman life and of Spartacus's life are as true to history as I could make them. Spartacus did lead a revolt from 73 B.C. to 71 B.C. Spartacus's wife escaped with him, although we do not know her name. Most of these details are taken from Plutarch, who wrote only a hundred years after Spartacus's revolt.

Thousands upon thousands of slaves joined Spartacus after the gladiators escaped from Mount Vesuvius. After a year, he led an army of nearly 100,000. The Roman army, which had conquered almost all of the known world, couldn't seem to defeat this ragtag army of slaves.

However, Spartacus knew that in the long run he could never defeat the Romans. He tried to stick to his plans to cross the Alps and escape Italy. But many of the gladiators became overimpressed with their own power and dreamed of overthrowing Rome altogether. Spartacus was unable to talk them into fleeing to their homelands.

Eventually, Spartacus's army was trapped in southern Italy. Spartacus was forced to fight a battle against the best and most powerful Roman army, which was led by the Roman general Crassus.

According to Plutarch, "On the day of the battle when Spartacus's horse was brought to him, he drew his sword and killed it, saying that the enemy had plenty of good horses which would be his if he won. And if he lost, he would not need a horse at all. Then he made straight for Crassus, himself, charging forward through the press of the weapons and wounded men. Though he did not reach Crassus, he cut down two centurions, who fell on him together. Finally, when his own men had taken to flight, he himself, surrounded by enemies, still stood his ground and died fighting to the last."

In order to teach other slaves a lesson, the Romans took a terrible revenge on the slaves they recaptured, crucifying six thousand of them along the Appian Way.

It is possible that Spartacus had studied Hannibal's tactics, but I did make up that part. It is true, however, that Hannibal tricked the Romans by tying torches onto the horns of cattle.

ELIZABETH LEVY, author of the ever-popular "Something Queer" mystery series, has been called "the Dorothy Sayers of the elementary set" by *Learning Magazine*. In addition to her numerous books for younger readers, Elizabeth Levy is well-respected for her young adult non-fiction as well, including *By-Lines, Profiles in Investigative Reporting* and *Politicians for the People* (with Mara Miller), published by Knopf.

Ms. Levy, who lives in New York City, completed her first marathon—the New York City Marathon—in October of 1979, running 26 miles and 385 yards in five hours and five minutes.